Children of the Northlights
by
Ingri and Edgar Parin d'Aulaire

CHILDREN
OF THE
NORTHLIGHTS

Ingri & Edgar Parin d'Aulaire
The Viking Press · New York

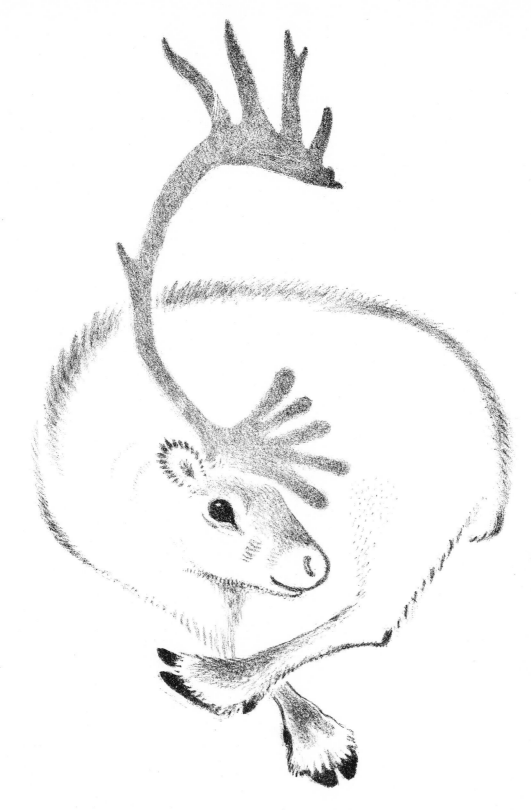

To Princess Ragnhild and Princess Astrid
of Norway

In the land of the Lapps the bears all snored in their winter sleep. But beautiful Northlights played on the sky and brightened the Polar Night. Wolves and foxes and hares
were wide awake. They all gazed up the mountain. For right on its tip there was a tent,
and there were hundreds of reindeer milling around outside it. The Lapps who owned the
herd must be hiding inside the tent, for from its top a wisp of light blue smoke crept out.

In front of the tent stood a small, black dog. He watched the herd while the Lapps slept. But it was dull to stand there alone, and when the Morning Star appeared, the dog barked to waken the Lapps. Almost at once a gayly colored star slipped out from the tent. This star was a cap, and behind the cap there was a boy. That was Lasse-Lapp. Right upon his heels his sister, Lappe-Lise, came crawling out. She always did just what her brother did, and that kept her busy from morning till night. They almost bumped into their reindeer, Silverside and Snowwhitedeer, but they did not have time for them right now.

8

For Lasse-Lapp always had funny ideas and now he had thought of a new one. And Lasse-Lapp and Lappe-Lise whispered and giggled; then they disappeared behind the tent.

After a while a bear came shambling along. He bumped into the tent and made a lot of noise, then he put his head right in through the tent door. That woke the Lapps in the tent. And the Lapp father, the Lapp mother, the three small boys, and the little girl all squeezed themselves out through the tent door to chase away the bear.

10

hen the bear laughed. "Pip, pip, now we fooled you," said Lise and Lasse as they peeped
ut from under the bear skin. They had taken the skin that hung behind the tent. At first
ne family was a little ashamed that they had been fooled so easily and had not remem-
ered that the bears were all sleeping, but then they laughed and danced a bear dance.
he Northlights gave them light, the dogs barked and made the music.

But the noise frightened the deer so that they ra
off down the mountain. Lise and Lasse put on the
skis, called their dogs, and started out to get th
reindeer back again. The deer had a good sta
and the children ran on so fast they did not eve
notice when the wind came up and the sno

began to drift. All of a sudden they were right in a raging snow storm, and all the deer were hidden by the snow. But the dogs smelled the herd; they barked and told the way. And Lise and Lasse followed the dogs without knowing where they were going. Then the dogs had to stop barking for the snow drifted right into their mouths.

13

And when Lise and Lasse came to a thicket of strange, twisted dwarf-birches, which the
had never seen before, they had no idea which way to go. So they crawled together to wa
for the storm to pass. The snow drifted over them, and soon it had covered them up
Only two small red noses and two black dogs' noses stuck out from a snowdrift.

When at last the snow storm had passed, the children shook themselves out of the snow. All around them the dwarf-birch forest began to move, and out from the snow came all the reindeer. For they, too, had been snowed under, and only their antlers had stuck out. And now Lise and Lasse saw that they had gone round in a ring in the snow storm and were lying right at their own tent door. They were shame-faced about it, but their brothers thought it was fun. They jumped around and teased them.

Lise and Lasse did not like that; they preferred to do the teasing themselves. But soon it was all forgotten. The dogs barked, the children played, and the reindeer all stood on their heads eating the moss under the deep snow. They were so greedy that soon there was no more moss left on the mountain. So the Lapps had to break camp and move with the herd to another mountain where the moss was still soft and untouched under the snow. The Lapp children loved to move and drive with their reindeer. Quickly the tent was taken down, and everything they owned was packed on sleds.

The baby had been sleeping beside the fire. It was wrapped in moss and fur and tightly tied up in its crib. But it did not like the ice-cold wind and started to whimper and wail. "If you stop crying, we will play reindeer," said Lasse and hitched himself up to the crib. He put his fingers up like antlers and almost thought he was a deer himself. He galloped and jumped through the snow while crib and baby swayed behind. Lise ran after and tried to catch the baby; she was afraid that Lasse might hurt it. She called and shouted but it did no good, for Lasse was a reindeer and did not understand Lapp. But when the father called to the children to come and catch the reindeer, Lasse at once was a Lapp boy again and Lise got the baby.

The dogs chased the herd together and the Lapps all swung their lassos, for none of the deer were tame enough to come by themselves. The father was a wealthy Lapp. He had almost a thousand reindeer. Still, the children knew every deer and had names for them all. The two nicest bucks, Silverside and Snow-whitedeer, belonged to Lise and Lasse. So Lasse caught Silverside and Lise caught Snowwhitedeer. The father caught a deer for each of the others but none for himself, for he would run on skis and lead the herd along. Lise was to hold the baby in the crib, and the little sister was to sit in the mother's lap.

All the other children were to drive their own reindeer. That was not so easy, for the sleds balanced on narrow keels, and once the reindeer had started they ran like the wind and never turned around to see if the drivers were still there. Silverside and Snowwhitedeer were wild and strong, and Lise and Lasse could not wait to be off. So they took good hold of the reins and jumped into their sleds.

The deer did not like to be hitched up at all, and did what they could to get rid of the children. Snowwhitedeer ran around in a ring until Lise was dizzy and almost fell out.

18

Silverside tried to scare Lasse away and came toward him with lowered horns. But Lasse just laughed and hid under his sled, and Silverside drummed with his hoofs on the keel.

19

Now the father started the herd, and off with a jerk ran Silverside and Snowwhitedeer, for they wanted to be first. The boys and the mother leapt into their sleds, but Lasse made a long furrow in the snow before he got into his.

He felt like racing with the whole world, even with the flaming sheet of Northlights that fluttered above his head. He jerked his arms and his legs and the points of his tarcap. This spurred Silverside on, and he ran still faster. And Snowwhitedeer and the rest of the reindeer raced along beside him. For a long while the only sound on the great plain was the tapping of thousands of reindeer feet.

By and by the deer got sleepy and lazy; the children had to sing and shout to keep them
from falling asleep on the spot. Snowwhitedeer and Silverside had tired themselves out
when they played at circus, so now they lagged behind. When they came to the new
camp place, the other deer were already busy testing the moss, and the tent had been pu

p again. It was nice and warm inside the tent, and they all crept together around the fire.
The father was the cook; he always kept the big pot of meat simmering. Lise was so
big she could help her mother sew their furs, and Lasse could carve wooden cups to
drink from. The ground was covered with twigs and with fur. That made their table,
their beds, and their seats. And the Polar Star gleamed through the top of the tent.

The dark winter lasted a long, long time, and Lasse and Lise began to wonder if the sun had quite forgotten them and the Polar night would never end. But at last one day the sun peeped timidly over the horizon. It had not much force, but the Lapp children thought they had never before seen such a lovely sun. And they all ran out to let it shine in their faces. The sun hid again almost at once, but next day it came back.

24

It stayed a little longer every day, and soon it was light from morning till night. Then it was time for Lise and Lasse to go to school. For every fall and spring Lapp children have to go to school in the village.

Once upon a time it was hard to get Lapp children to school. The Lapps were great bear-hunters and were famous all over the world as wizards, but they were afraid of the school. The teacher had to come for the children himself, and they ran off and hid in the mountains. So he caught them with his lasso, just as he caught his reindeer, and dragged them with him.

But that was long ago, and now Lise and Lasse hardly could wait for school to begin. They were so eager for the marvels of the village that they did not mind even leaving their reindeer. Lise and Lasse told the dogs to take good care of them while they were away. Then they stowed their Sunday suits inside their furs, took leave of their family, and set off. They went on their skis, uphill and downhill, but mostly downhill, until they came to a wide river. There they sat down to wait for the schoolmaster. Soon they heard tinkling bells and saw a huge horse trotting down on the ice of the river. That was the schoolmaster's. He was out with his sledge picking up schoolchildren, and he already had his sledge full. Lise and Lasse just stood and gaped at the sight of the horse and so many children, but the teacher reached out, grabbed them, and put them on top of the others in the sledge. Soon Lise and Lasse had forgotten their shyness. The children chattered and the ice creaked as the horse trotted toward the village.

At last the river made a big bend, and there was the village. Many small houses were scattered along the river bank, and there were many people but no reindeer. The first house they reached was steaming and smoking. That was the bathhouse, the teacher said.

nd he sent the children in to get a bath before coming to town. Inside an old woman was
usy making steam. She welcomed the children and told them to take off their furs and
rawl up on the shelves under the roof. There they sat in the steam clouds like angels in
he sky, and the old woman made it warmer and warmer by throwing water on red-hot
tones. When the children were themselves as hot as the steam, she rubbed them and

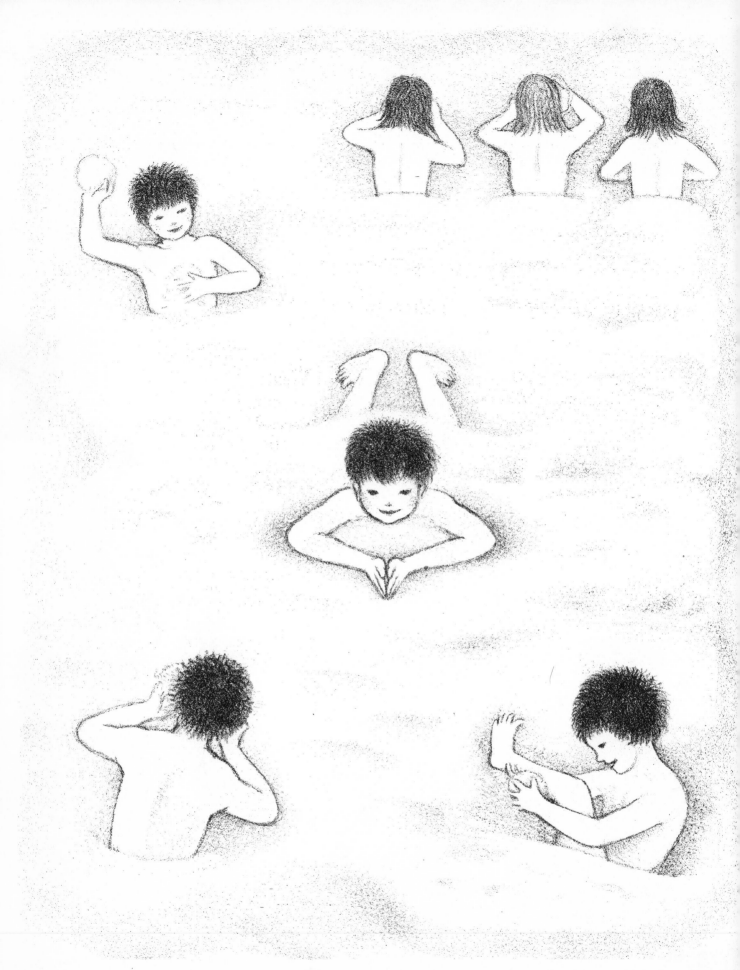

sent them all out to roll in the snow. Then Lise and Lasse ran to the schoolmaster's hous
and put on their fine suits of blue cloth with gayly coloured borders, for in the village
was like Sunday every day in the week.

28

nd the teacher gave them a whole mountain of fresh hay. They pulled and patted it
nd made something like bird's nests. The birds' nests they put into their shoes. That
ept their feet so warm they did not even need stockings.

Meanwhile all the village children stood gazing in the doorway. At first Lise and Lasse
ere a little shy, they had never thought there could be so many children in the world.
ut soon they had made friends with them and learned all the village games.

Every day they all went to school. The teacher taught them not to chatter and not t[o]
squat, but to sit quietly on benches and listen to him while he taught them to read and t[o]
draw beautiful letters. He also told about the world that was big and round. They coul[d]
see it for themselves; they lived almost at its top.

30

But it was not long before Lise and Lasse began to get homesick. Every day they looked at the snow-bare spot on the mountain, for when it had grown to the shape of a waving man their parents had promised to come. And one morning there really was a man on the slope; he was waving both arms and legs to them.

And there, on the ridge of the mountain, they saw a crowd of merry Lapps. There wer

Lise's and Lasse's parents and some of their friends. They all were bringing their babie

for christening in the village church. Now they sat in a ring, betting on who could driv

down the slope in the craziest way.

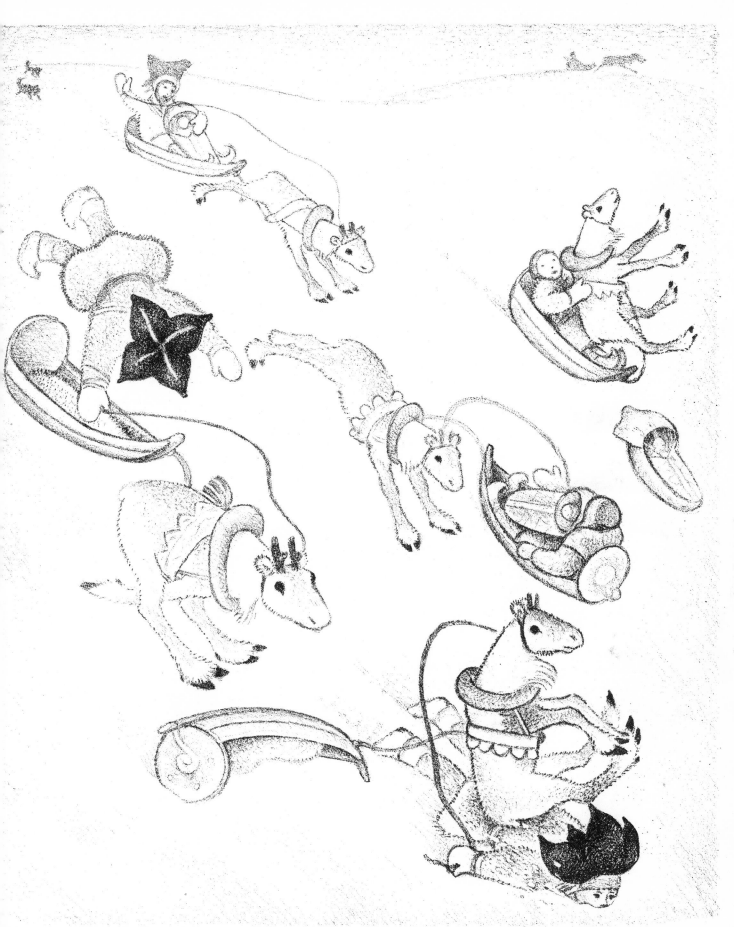

Then they jumped into their sleds, and the reindeer swept down the slope like light-ing. But some of the sleds were swifter still and caught up with the deer. Lise's and Lasse's parents were the funniest of all. The mother's deer was upset and fell right onto her lap; the father had both deer and sled on top of him.

But the cribs with the babies fell out of the sleds. All by themselves they tumbled down the hill and were the first to arrive in the village. Then came Lapps and reindeer helter-skelter. The Lapps laughed and shouted and picked up their babies. The babies had not even been hurt, they were so well packed in furs and moss. "I am so glad, so glad," said both Lise and Lasse, and they smiled over their whole bodies as they ran to greet their parents. Eagerly Lasse helped his father tie up the reindeer, and he brought each deer a lump of frozen moss, for no moss grew under the snow in the village.

Lise and her mother sat down together and unpacked the baby from its crib. When Lise saw her baby brother, she clapped her hands together. For the first time he was fully dressed up and looked just like a tiny grown-up Lapp. Then the church bell began to ring, and all the Lapps took the babies on their arms and stalked in through the church door. Some of the babies were so big that they screamed and kicked, for they did not want to be carried.

After church there were christening parties all over the village. Everyone who would bring along a present for the babies was invited. Lise's and Lasse's tiny brother got a beautiful reindeer. It had pitch-black hoofs, so they named it Blackhoof. When the baby grew up, Lasse would teach him to drive it.

Now Lise and Lasse could drive home with their parents, for school was over for that spring. They did not even know where home was right now, for the tent had been moved many times since they went off. They were so happy to think they would soon see their sister and brothers and their dogs and Silverside and Snowwhitedeer and all the other reindeer again that they did not mind leaving their village friends. And in a long row, with the father at the head leading the way, they drove up from the valley and back to the mountain wind.

The dogs were wild with joy to see Lise and Lasse again; they almost ate them up. And Silverside was gentle and stood still. He even let Lasse pat him. But perhaps he was jus vain about his horns. For all the reindeer were getting new antlers. They would stand still and rub the knob with their hind feet, and where they rubbed a new branch woul

row out. There were lots of tiny reindeer calves that had come while Lise and Lasse were
way. And the sun was warm and the snowbirds twittered and Lasse and Lise found
ussy-willow buds behind the tent.

Listen," said Lise to Lasse, "each tree sings with its own voice."

And now came the big event of the year. The sun was burning stronger and stronger, and the Lapps had to hurry on. They wanted to reach the coast before the sun had licked up all the snow and made the reindeer too lazy to move. They would stay on the coast the whole long summer when the sun never sets, and let their reindeer eat the fresh green grass around the shores. For several weeks they would be driving. They would sleep at noon when the sun was high and would move at night when the snow was hard and could carry them. Lise and Lasse and their family set off gayly. But in the fall they would be still happier to return to their mountains.

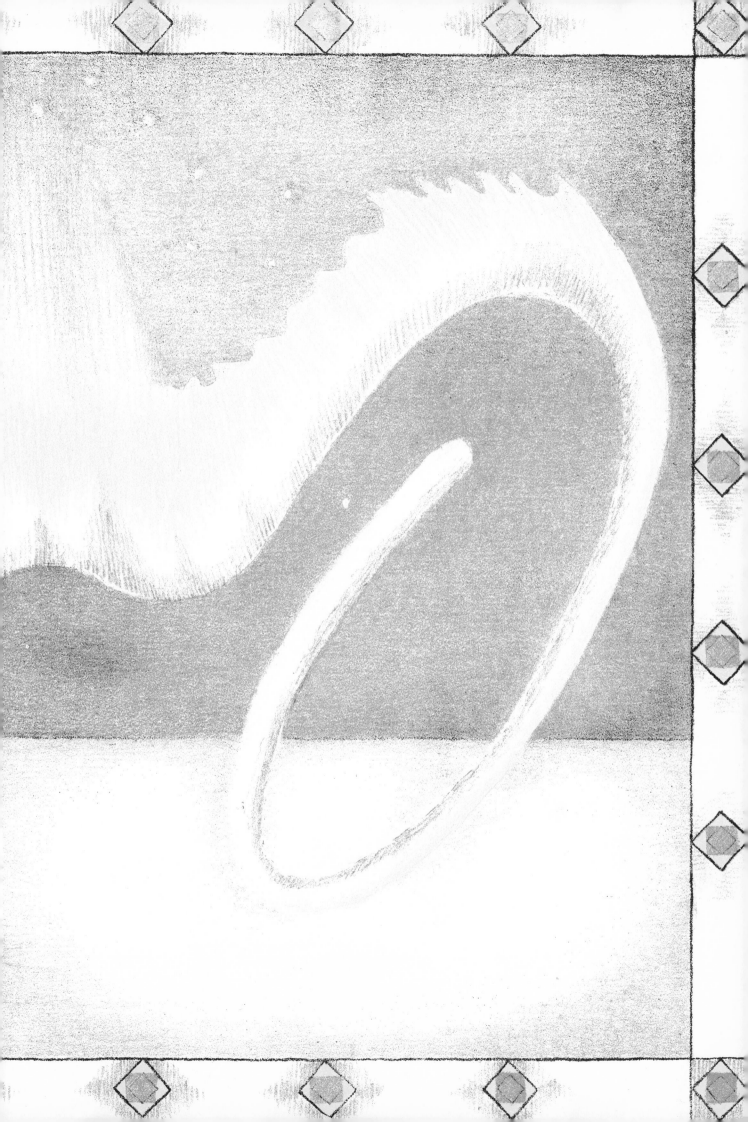